Membership Card

Name

Nickname

School

Age

The Mystery of the Old Knife

by M. J. Cosson

Perfection Learning®

Cover and Inside Illustrations: Michael A. Aspengren

For information, contact
Perfection Learning® Corporation,
1000 North Second Avenue, P.O. Box 500,
Logan, Iowa 51546-0500.
Tel: 1-800-831-4190
Fax: 1-800-543-2745
PB ISBN-13: 978-0-7891-2846-1 ISBN-10: 0-7891-2846-2
RLB ISBN-13: 978-0-7807-9699-7 ISBN-10: 0-7807-9699-3

6 7 8 9 10 11 PP 12 11 10 09 08 07

Table of Contents

Introduction

Abe, Ben, Gabe, Toby, and Ty live in a large city. There isn't much for kids to do. There isn't even a park close by.

Their neighborhood is made up of
apartment houses and trailer parks.
Gas stations and small shops stand
where the parks and grass used to be.
And there aren't many houses with
big yards.

Ty and Abe live in an apartment complex. Next door is a large vacant lot. It is full of brush, weeds, and trash. A path runs across the lot. On the other side is a trailer park. Ben and Toby live there.

Across the street from the trailer park is a big gray house. Gabe lives in the top apartment of the house.

The five boys have known one another since they started school. But they haven't always been friends.

The other kids say the boys have cooties. And the other kids won't touch them with a ten-foot pole. So Abe, Ben, Gabe, Toby, and Ty have formed their own club. They call it the Kooties Club.

Here's how to join. If no one else will have anything to do with you, you're in.

The boys call themselves the Koots for short. Ben's grandma calls his grandpa an *old coot.* And Ben thinks his grandpa is pretty cool. So if he's an old coot, Ben and his friends must be young koots.

The Koots play ball and hang out with one another. But most of all, they look for mysteries to solve.

Chapter 1

The Find

"Cut that out!" yelled Gabe. He rubbed his eyes.

Abe turned around. He had thrown dirt in Gabe's face again.

"Oops, sorry," Abe said. He put the shovel down. "I guess I'm getting tired."

"Give it to me," said Ty. He jumped into the hole and picked up the shovel.

The hole was about four feet deep and four feet wide.

"It needs to be a lot deeper. And wider," Toby said. "Keep digging, Ty."

While Ty dug, Abe held the flashlight. The Koots sat around the edge of the hole. They thought about how this whole thing had started.

The Koots had wanted a place of their own. Nobody had a garage. Nobody had a basement. Nobody even had a real yard.

There was no place to meet that was private. It was going to be a long summer. Then Toby had an idea.

What about the empty lot?" he asked.

"What about it?" Gabe asked.

"Nobody uses it for much. Except to dump stuff," Toby said.

"It's just a dirty lot. With junk on it. It has rats too," said Ty.

11

"Yeah. I saw a big one there," Abe said. He held out his hands to show the size. "That rat was as big as a cat," he said.

Ben stared at Abe. The look said that he didn't believe him. "A kitten maybe," Ben said. He looked back at Toby. "But there are no trees," he added. "Where would we build a clubhouse?"

"Who said anything about trees?" asked Toby.

"We could clean it up," suggested Ben.

"That would be nice of us," said Toby. "But that's not what I have in mind." Toby looked at each of the Koots.

"What I have in mind is a cave," he went on. "We could dig a cave and put

stuff over it. Nobody would know it's there. It would be a secret place. And it would be cool."

"It would be dirty," Abe said.

"We can line it with cardboard," Toby said.

"Somebody will walk on it and fall in," Ben said. "Then we'll be in trouble . . . again."

"We'll use that old piece of fence for the cover. We can pile stuff on the top. We'll make it look like a pile of junk. But it will really be the top of the cave. We'll be the only ones who know what's really under it," Toby said.

"People will see us digging it out," said Ben. "Everybody will know."

"We'll do it when it's dark," Toby said proudly. He had an answer for everything.

13

The Koots all looked at one another.

"It's our only chance. We can call it the Kootie Cave," Gabe said.

"The Kooties Club Cave," Ben added.

"The Kooties Club Cool Cave," Ty added.

"Instead of a clubhouse, we'll have a club cave," Abe said.

"Who has a shovel?" asked Ty.

"My landlady does," said Gabe. "I'll get it. Let's meet at the lot at 8 o'clock. It's almost dark by then."

So the Koots had started digging. When Ty got tired, Gabe dug. When he was tired, Toby dug. Then Ben dug. Then Abe dug. It was then Ty's turn. They took turns holding the flashlight too.

Now the Koots were sitting on the edge of the hole thinking what a neat

14

club cave they would have. Ty was digging in the hole. It was getting deep. But it needed to be wider. So he scooped dirt from the side.

Something fell off his shovel with the dirt. It was long and brown. Ty picked it up.

The thing was hard to see in the dark. So Abe pointed the flashlight at it. It looked like a large, rusty knife. Dirt stuck to its sides. The other Koots all jumped in for a closer look.

"What is it?" asked Ben.

"I think it's an old knife," answered Ty. He held it up.

"Let me see," said Gabe. He grabbed at it.

"No, I'm looking at it," said Ty. He yanked it away.

15

"Yeow!" Gabe yelled. He looked down at his hand. Blood seeped from his palm. "It's sharp!" he said.

Gabe's hand was dripping blood. His face was white.

"Gotta go," he said. "Help me out of this hole."

"Hold your hand up. It won't bleed so much," Toby offered.

The Koots helped Gabe climb out of the hole. Then Ben helped Gabe to his house. Gabe's dad was home. He took Gabe to the clinic.

16

Chapter 2

The Questions

By the time Gabe got to the clinic, it was 10 p.m.

"What did you cut this on?" asked the doctor.

"I don't know," answered Gabe. He trembled as the doctor cleaned the wound. He didn't watch the doctor put in the stitches.

"You don't know?" The doctor gave Gabe a suspicious look.

Gabe looked up. "I guess it was a knife," he said softly.

Gabe's dad looked at him. "What were you doing with a knife?" he asked. "Were you in a fight?"

"No," Gabe said quickly. "We found it. I just wanted to look at it. And Ty pulled it away from me."

"Where did you find the knife?" the doctor asked.

"In a yard," Gabe said. He didn't want to tell about the digging. He didn't want to give away the secret of the club cave.

"Where is the knife now?" Gabe's dad asked.

"My friends have it, I guess," Gabe replied.

18

"What kind of knife is it?" the doctor asked.

"Old," Gabe answered.

"Big or little?" his dad asked.

"Pretty big," Gabe replied.

"Could be a hunting knife," his dad said.

"Could be a murder weapon too," Gabe said.

"Could be gang-related," the doctor said. "Your friends should give it to the police."

The doctor finished stitching the wound. He leaned against the counter and studied Gabe's chart.

"Was the knife rusty?" the doctor asked.

"I guess so," answered Gabe. "It was all brown."

"Better give you a tetanus shot too," said the doctor.

Gabe moaned. "That's not going to make my hand feel better," he said.

"No, it won't," said his dad. "But the sting of the shot will take your mind off your sore hand." He laughed. The doctor laughed too. Gabe just frowned at them both.

Chapter 3

Time to Go

After Gabe left, the Koots stopped digging. They sat in the hole and studied the knife. Carefully, they passed it around.

The knife looked very old. The wooden handle was gone. There was just the big, thick blade. A stub of metal hinted at where the handle used to be.

"What do you think it was used for?"
Ben asked.

"Hunting," Abe said, nodding his head.

"Fighting," Ty said, imitating a
warrior he had seen on TV.

"Maybe stabbing," Toby guessed.

"Killing," Ben said. "Definitely killing."

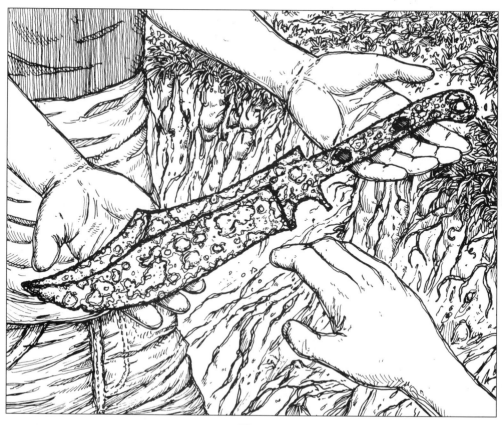

"Maybe we're sitting on the body," Ty said.

"I—I have to get h—home," Abe stuttered. He jumped up. "My dad is looking for me."

"Me too," said the other Koots. They hurried out of the hole.

"Let's leave the knife in the hole for tonight," Ben said.

Ty agreed. He threw the knife back into the hole.

The Koots pulled the fence over the opening. They piled weeds, sticks, and old cans and bottles on the fence. In the dark, they couldn't tell there was a hole under the fence. Of course, there was the mound of dirt beside the hole. It looked just like a new grave—or an old one that had been dug up.

23

Chapter 4

Koots Need Help

The next morning, the Koots met at Gabe's house.

"How's the hand?" asked Ty.

"Six stitches," said Gabe. He held up his bandaged hand. "And a tetanus shot." Gabe acted like he was in pain.

"Where's the knife?" Gabe asked.

"In the hole," Ben replied.

"It's covered with the fence. You can't even tell," said Abe.

"Except for the new grave . . . er, dirt," said Toby.

"What did you tell them? I mean about how you got cut?" asked Ben.

"I said I got cut with a knife." Gabe looked at each of the Koots. "Don't worry, I didn't tell about the hole. I said we found the knife in a yard. They didn't ask which yard. The doctor said to take it to the police."

"Yeah," said Toby. "We thought about that. It might be from a murder."

"It would be a really old murder," Abe said. "That knife has been in the ground for a long time."

"I know!" said Ben. "Let's take the knife to Mr. Dodge. He used to be a police officer. He can tell us what to do with it."

"Good thinking, Sherlock," said Ty. "Let's go."

25

The Koots walked over to the lot. Four Koots stood guard while Ty crawled into the hole. After he got the knife, the other boys replaced the cover.

No one had walked by. No one saw Ty go in or come out of the hole.

The Koots trooped to Mr. Dodge's apartment. They knocked.

"It's open!" yelled Mr. Dodge.

The Koots filed into the dark apartment. It always took a minute for their eyes to adjust. Mr. Dodge was used to the dark. He was blind. And that's the way his world always was.

"What's up, fellas?"

"We have something to show you," said Ben. "It's a knife."

"Be careful, Mr. Dodge," said Gabe. "I already got six stitches and a shot from that thing."

Mr. Dodge held out his hands, palms up. "Put it here," he said.

Ty carefully placed the knife in his hands. Mr. Dodge turned the knife over. He felt the dirty metal sides.

"Where did you boys get this?" he asked.

The Koots explained.

"I think you have a relic here," said Mr. Dodge.

"Oh, we thought it was a knife," said Abe matter-of-factly.

Mr. Dodge smiled. "It is a knife, Abe," he said. "A *relic* is something very old," continued Mr. Dodge. "It's something from times past. This feels like it could be a bowie knife."

"What's a 'booey' knife?" asked Ty.

"Have you heard of the Alamo?" asked Mr. Dodge. The boys just looked at their friend.

"A long time ago, there was a man named Jim Bowie. He became a legend of the Old West. He did a lot of interesting things. Some were good. Some were bad.

"When he was a kid, he rode alligators," Mr. Dodge continued. "He bought and sold land. And he bought and sold slaves. He was a friend to the Indians. And he was in many fights. He killed many men with his special knife."

Mr. Dodge turned the knife over in his hands again. "He's best known for two things. He died at the battle of the Alamo. He and others were trying to free Texas from Mexico. And he and his brother invented the bowie knife.

"Back in the mid-1800s," Mr. Dodge said, "every man who hunted or lived in the Wild West had a bowie knife. In fact, the knives were found all over America."

"Do you think this was his knife?" asked Ben.

"I doubt it," answered Mr. Dodge. "But it feels like it might be that old."

The Koots all looked at one another.

"I have an idea," said Mr. Dodge. "I have a friend who teaches at city college. He's an *archaeologist.*"

"A what? An ark-key what?" asked Toby.

"You say it *ark-ee-all-oh-just,*" explained Mr. Dodge. "He studies things from the past. He studies relics. I'd like to have him look at this."

The Koots looked at one another. They nodded.

"Sure," said Ben. "Go ahead and call him."

"One more thing," said Mr. Dodge. "Don't dig anymore. Wait until you talk to my friend. There may be more *artifacts* there."

Chapter 5

Dr. Doug

The Koots waited for three days. Each
day, they checked in with Mr. Dodge.
Each day, he said his friend had the
knife. But his friend hadn't gotten back
to him.

"He's busy," said Mr. Dodge.

"He has our knife," said Ty.

"And we can't even dig in our cave,"
added Abe.

"Just wait," said Mr. Dodge.

Finally on the fourth day, Mr. Dodge had news. When the Koots went to see him, his friend was there.

"Boys, this is Dr. Doug Evans," Mr. Dodge said.

"Call me Dr. Doug," the man said.

Everyone shook hands with Dr. Doug—except Gabe. He held up his bandaged hand. "You might want to see my stitches," said Gabe, "since you're a doctor. I got them from that knife."

"I'm not that kind of doctor, Gabe," said Dr. Doug. "I'm a doctor of archaeology. I study old things."

"Right," said a disappointed Gabe. "Relics."

"Artifacts," Ty said.

"Exactly," said Dr. Doug. "I do digs."

"So do we," said Abe. "We were digging when we found the knife."

"Exactly," said Dr. Doug. "Did you find anything else? Any broken dishes? Any other tools?"

"We dug up some junk," said Ben.

"Will you boys show me where you found the knife?"

"It's a secret," said Toby.

"It might be an important historic site," said Dr. Doug. "Your knife is very old. At least 150 years old."

Dr. Doug picked up a piece of soft cloth. He opened it. Inside was a shiny knife.

"That's like our knife," said Toby.

"But newer," Ty added.

"This is your knife," said Dr. Doug. I have done some things to restore it."

33

"Wow!" said all the Koots.

"It would be very helpful if you would show me where you got it," said Dr. Doug. "We may want to do a dig there."

The Koots were quiet.

"You would be helping people learn more about history," said Dr. Doug.

No one said anything.

At last, Ben asked, "Will you excuse us?" The Koots all walked out of Mr. Dodge's apartment. They closed the door.

"What do you think?" asked Ben.

"Good-bye, Kootie Club Cave," Toby said.

"We'd be helping people learn," Ben said.

"We can do our own digging," Ty said.

34

"What about the body?" Abe asked.

"What body?" Gabe asked.

"The one that might have been buried with the knife," Ty said.

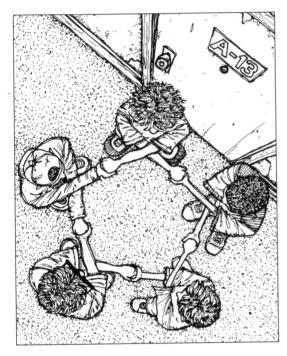

The Koots talked some more. At last, they did the Kootie handshake. Then they went back inside.

Gabe spoke for the Koots. "Okay, it's a deal. But one thing," he said.

"Shoot," said Dr. Doug.

"Can we help?"

"Of course!" laughed Dr. Doug. "I was going to ask you."

Chapter 6

The Dig

Dr. Doug checked with the city. He found out that nothing had ever been built on the lot. The city owned it. At one time, it was going to be a small park. But the park never got built.

"This is very strange for a lot in the city," he said. "Most lots have had buildings on them. This might be a dumping ground. It might even be sacred ground. That would be great."

"Of course it's a dumping ground," Ty said. "Everybody dumps trash there."

"What's sacred ground?" asked Abe.

"It's ground that people in old times kept for special uses. It could even be a burial ground," Dr. Doug said.

Abe and Ty looked at each other and turned a little green. They just knew that soon they would be digging up bodies.

By the end of the week, the Koots were digging again. Only this digging was much slower.

College students worked with the Koots. Everybody dug. Even Dr. Doug dug. So far, they hadn't found much— just some jars, bottles, and other junk.

The lot had been roped off. The whole lot was a big grid. There were lines every few feet. One student had graph paper. She drew things on it.

37

Instead of large shovels, they used spoons and small shovels called *trowels*. They dug tiny spoonfuls. Then they put the dirt in a bucket.

When they found something, they didn't pick it up. They got a little brush. They brushed off the top. They brushed all around it.

Next they called the student with the graph paper. She measured exactly where

the object was. Then she drew it on the graph paper. It was a lot of work.

"I feel like a little kid," complained Ben. "Like I'm digging in a sandpile."

"We need our little trucks," said Ty.

"I used to have a dump truck," Abe said. "I wonder if I still have it."

"Yeah, we might as well be playing cars," Toby said.

"We found that knife in one night," Gabe said.

"I know," said Ty. "We could dig up this lot in no time if we didn't have to use spoons."

"But we might miss a jar," said Toby.

"Ha, ha," said Ben.

Just then Dr. Doug walked by. "We'll have to dig deeper. The good stuff may be a few feet down," he said. "Good job, boys. Keep digging."

All the Koots were thinking the same thing. They were spending the summer digging with spoons. It was hot and dirty work. And it was slow.

They could be in their secret club cave. It would be cool. It would be fun. It would be better than this. If only they hadn't found the knife. If only they hadn't asked Mr. Dodge for help.

Chapter 7

To Dig or Not to Dig

There was one good thing about the dig. The Koots didn't have to dig unless they wanted to. Every day, the college kids dug. Every day, Dr. Doug dug. But the Koots could play ball in the parking lot. They could swim at the city pool. They could listen to mystery tapes at Mr. Dodge's. The Koots only dug when they had nothing else to do.

Of course, they checked in each day. They didn't want to miss anything. Most of the good stuff had been found near the Koots cave. So the dig was getting deeper there.

"Soon they'll find the body," Gabe said. "Maybe we'd better start helping some more."

"I don't want to be there when they find the body," said Abe.

"Me neither," Ty added.

"Okay, you stay home," Ben said. "Tomorrow, I'm digging."

"Me too," chimed Gabe.

"Me too," Toby said.

Abe and Ty looked at the Koots. They didn't want to miss anything either.

"Okay, me too," Abe said.

"Yeah, me too," Ty said.

Chapter 8

"It's a . . ."

Two more days went by. They were long, boring days. The Koots dug and dusted. They dusted and dug.

One of the college kids found an old bullet. Toby and Ty found arrowheads. There were lots of arrowheads about two feet down.

"This might have been an old hunting ground," Dr. Doug said. "Before the city was ever here."

"That makes sense," Ben said.

Dr. Doug smiled. "Let's dig some more," he said.

After Dr. Doug walked away, Toby said, "I see why they call him Dr. Doug. All he ever does is dig."

"Yeah, he's Dr. Dug, Dug, Dug," Abe said.

"No," said Ben. "He's Dr. Dig, Dig, Dig. Dug means you're done."

"Yup," said Gabe. "He's Dr. Dig."

Thonk! Gabe's spoon hit something hard.

"Probably a rock," he said.

Gabe took the brush. He started dusting. The thing that he hit was long and thin. It was yellow. He dug a little more. He dusted. There was one just like it next to it. Then there was another. And another.

"It's a rib cage!" Ben shouted.

"It's a . . ."

Chapter 9

Old Bones

"This is very close to where the knife fell out," Ty said. "It could be the body that was buried with the knife."

"Dr. Doug!" all the Koots yelled together.

Dr. Doug came over. He had to step carefully around the diggers.

"What's up, boys?" he asked.

The Koots pointed to the rib cage.

"Wow," said Dr. Doug. Soon all the college kids were looking too.

"This is right by where we found the knife," said Gabe. "We think it could be the body that got buried with the knife."

"Okay, boys," said Dr. Doug. "Why don't you let Jim, Mary, and me work here. If this is a human, we may have to stop. It could be a sacred burial ground."

"Then what will happen?" asked Ben.

"I'll need to tell the city. They'll move everything out. Or build a wall around this lot. This might be why nothing was ever built here."

The Koots looked at one another. Where would they play if the city built a wall around the lot?

"This could be a graveyard," Ty said.

"We've been playing in a graveyard!" Abe gasped.

"Worse than that," said Ben. "We've been digging in a graveyard!"

Dr. Doug and his two students started to brush the dirt off the rib cage. They worked very slowly. Much more slowly than the Koots had been working. They worked until dark. Then they turned on a light and worked some more.

At last, it was time to quit. Everyone was tired. Still, only the rib cage showed above the dirt. Dr. Doug covered the area with a tarp.

"The tarp will keep it clean and safe until morning," Dr. Doug said.

"See you all back here at 6 a.m. sharp," he said.

48

The Koots walked home. Ben, Gabe, and Toby went one way. Ty and Abe went the other way. After Abe went into his apartment, Ty ran up the stairs to his apartment.

That night Ty had a dream. The bones sat up in the graveyard. They'd been waiting for many years. At last, someone had found them. They stood up and walked around. They were looking for something. Where was the knife? The bones started walking toward the apartments.

Ty screamed. He woke himself up. He lay very still in bed.

I don't have the knife, he thought. The bones won't come here.

But he didn't go back to sleep for a long time.

49

Chapter 10

The Real Story

The next day, Ty was glad to see the bones still in the ground.

Dr. Doug and the college kids dug and dusted. The Koots just watched. At last, they could see the spine. Then the hip bones. But the body was funny. It looked all twisted.

"Must have been a bad death," said Gabe. "I thought they were always laid out straight."

"Maybe this happened after it was buried," Toby said.

"Maybe it was buried alive," Ty said. "Maybe it got twisted, trying to get out of the ground."

"I think what we have here," said Dr. Doug, "is not a human."

Gabe bent over the bones for a closer look. "Is that a tail?" he asked.

"Exactly," said Dr. Doug. "Let's work on the head a little."

Dr. Doug and his students moved to the other end.

"Better yet," said Dr. Doug. "Let's let the boys do this."

He smiled up at the Koots. He handed Ty a brush.

51

"Be my guest," he said.

Ty took the brush. Gabe got one too. So did Abe. Toby and Ben did the same.

The Koots began to brush the dirt from the skull. They brushed the forehead. They brushed around the eye sockets. Then they brushed around the nose.

It wasn't human. The nose was too big. The forehead was too wide. It looked like a big cat.

"I think it's a big cat," said Ben.

"Exactly," said Dr. Doug. "Keep brushing, boys. Brush that part."

He pointed to the side of the cat. It was close to the big hole. The Koots brushed. Slowly they dug up the cat's shoulder blade. There was a gash in it.

"See this?" asked Dr. Doug. "This is where the knife struck."

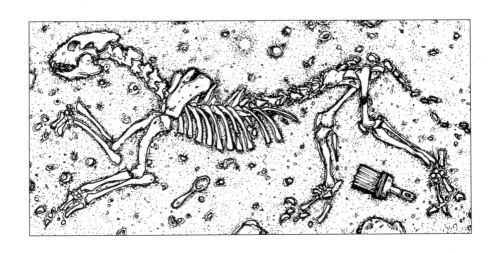

"I see," Gabe said. "Someone threw a knife at this cat."

"They were hunting for food," Abe said.

"Or maybe it attacked them. They were trying to protect themselves," Toby said.

"It might be a mountain lion," Ty said.

"Or a panther," Ben said.

"The knife went in the shoulder," Abe said.

"But the cat wasn't killed," Dr. Doug said.

"The cat ran off with the knife in it," Toby said.

"It lost a lot of blood," Ty said.

"Finally it died," Ben said. "The knife was still in it."

"When we dug the hole, we hit the knife," Toby said.

"And we've been digging all this time," Gabe started.

"And this isn't a graveyard for people," Abe added.

"It's a hunting ground," Ty said.

"Or it just used to be woods," Ben said.

"The big cat came here to die," Abe finished.

"Exactly," said Dr. Doug.

Epilogue

After the case was solved, Dr. Doug and his students went back to the university. The lot was all cleaned up. It looked good. It would have been a good time for the city to make it into a park. But it didn't happen.

Some of the neighbors made it into a garden. After all, the dirt was all turned over. It was ready to be planted. They grew beans, flowers, and pumpkins.

The Koots forgot about their clubhouse. Who wanted a clubhouse in the middle of a garden? Who wanted a cave where a big cat had died?

The next year, the neighbors forgot about the garden. People started throwing junk on the lot again.

The Koots got to keep the knife. But their parents wouldn't let them keep it for themselves.

The Koots gave it to the college, where it was put into a display case. The arrowheads, bullets, and other things from the lot were put there too. The note by the knife read

This bowie knife killed a mountain lion. It was found with the mountain lion's body. The knife is 150 years old.

Donated by Abe, Ben, Gabe, Toby, and Ty—the Kooties Club